About the Author

Debbi Voisey has had short stories published in *Ad Hoc*, *The Bath Short Story Award*, *Ellipsis*, *Reflex*, *Litro* and others. She has been longlisted and shortlisted in several competitions, including *Bath Short Story Award*, *Flash 500*, and *Reflex Fiction*.

The 10:25 was shortlisted in the Bath Novella-in-Flash Award in 2018, and she has another Novella-in-Flash forthcoming later in 2021.

Only About Love

DEBBI VOISEY

Fairlight Books

First published by Fairlight Books 2021

Fairlight Books
Summertown Pavilion, 18–24 Middle Way, Oxford, OX2 7LG

A CIP catalogue record for this book is available from the
British Library

1 2 3 4 5 6 7 8 9 10

ISBN 978-1-914148-00-2

www.fairlightbooks.com

Printed and bound in Great Britain by Clays Ltd.

Designed by Sara Wood
Illustrated by Sam Kalda

For Leon Jones 1941 - 2019
No matter what, always my dad

Contents

Reversing Sensor   11

Breaking Dad   14

All the Things Frank Will and Will Not Do   15

Black, White and Red   17

Wonky Stocking Seams   19

The Future   22

Making a Baby   24

That Rare 0.03%   27

Whistle   32

I Just Can't Help Believing   34

Urban Love Affair – The First Time   38

Gypsy Toast   41

The End   43

Bus Notices (And What They Really Mean)   45

Not All Heroes Wear Capes   49

Waiting for the Slam   51

Heatwave   53

Affairs of the Heart   56

A Decision Has to be Made   58
Gone   61
Hairy, Tickling Toes   64
His Lover   66
Innings   69
The Man of the House   72
Mondays Without Mick   75
Items in an Adulterer's Holdall   76
Deceipt/Receit   79
Searching   81
Time Bomb   83
Funeral   86
Progressive Regression   88
Fly Away   91
Two Heartbeats   94
He Needs Nothing   96
A Dipping Cuppa   97
Frank's Hands   99
In Dreams   100
Things Frank Loves   102
Flounder   104
Loss   107
DNR   108
The Doorway Through
Which Your Heart Is Destroyed   112
I'll Never Forget I Love You   115

The Thing They Don't Talk About   118

Let Forever Be Now   120

Don't Fear the Wolf or:

The Slow Devouring of Frank   122

Weather   124

Dad-Shaped Hole   126

Letting Him Go   128

Only About Love   131

Whistle Stop   132

Now I'm Found   134

Reversing Sensor

Rushing full pelt through life like you're a superhero with wings or at least a cape or an anorak without your arms in going forward, forward, forward through your childhood listening to the wireless where posh men's voices are telling you about lands far away but not too far away over the sea where people are dying and being tortured by the Nazis and your dad's there and you worry about him and wonder when or if he's coming back but then he *is* back and your mum says not to bother him let him sit with his pipe but you see his eyes watching you and he calls you an imp, an urchin, a fucking bugger and you've never heard your dad talk like that or seen that look in his eyes before like the one he has when he won't let you leave the table until you've stuffed every morsel on the plate down you because he's seen people with bones sticking out of paper-thin skin who were vomiting up their insides through starvation so you choke it all down and swear at him the way you heard him swear and he puts carbolic soap in your mouth and scrapes it hard until your teeth are covered in it and you swallow it and retch then spin forward, forward, forward to when you're a young man and you meet your wife who loves you more than you deserve which is obvious by the way she holds you when you cry at night because you remember the beatings and before you know it you have two kids of your own who you show love to by feeding them but not with force like he fed you and you never beat them unless you count the times you pretend to your wife that you're disciplining them but you do it with a soft slipper and you secretly laugh at their secret laughs before spinning forward, forward, forward into middle age where you're getting ready to go to your dad's funeral even though you swear you hate him but you break down and sob because you don't hate him you don't and you spin forward, forward, forward into old age where you watch your sister die screaming from Alzheimer's and it's terrifying so you hope you pray you don't get it but you have to go to a clinic where someone tells you a phone number and asks you questions like who's the Prime Minister and what was that phone number I told you five minutes ago and you know David Cameron is the Prime Minister but you don't remember her telling you a phone number so you spin backward, backward, backward and try to ignore it and try to pretend it's not happening even when your wife asks you to promise to give up driving when you know the time's right because you're getting stressed and you can't remember the way to anywhere even though you've been a professional driver all your life and you know the country like the back of your hand so you say yes you promise to give up but you don't ever want to give up but one day you're driving backward, backward, backward and even though that alarm thing is beeping and getting quicker and quicker you somehow crash into the car behind and you know it, you sense it, the time is coming.

Breaking Dad

Through the crackled panel of the door you see him lying at the foot of the stairs; a grisly painting in mosaic. Blue of the pyjamas he's been wearing since Thursday, white of the skin that never sees sunshine, and crimson of something terrible... up near his head. The picture is all joined together like the tiles on an ancient temple's floor. Beautiful but damaged.

Yesterday he'd been more difficult than usual. Said that without her he didn't know what to do with himself. Every morning he got out of bed and just wanted to die. You shrugged it off. He's always been melodramatic. Even before the heavy curtain came to lock down his memories.

Mum is in hospital and your only job was not to break dad while she was gone.

You fumble with your key in the door, your heart pounding.

All the Things Frank Will and Will Not Do

Frank will be born one of seven children and live in a house where the first one down in the morning will be the best dressed and most fed. He'll spend his childhood eating soggy toast and dodging his father's backhanders, and all his siblings will adore him.

Frank will wear short trousers and scuff his knees, but climbing and falling out of trees will harden him.

Frank will have many girlfriends, and many fights with boys – and later men – because of it.

Frank will be the funniest boy in school, the coolest man at the factory, the most handsome man in the pub, but he'll never know it. He'll spend most of his time thinking he's not good enough, and the rest of his time proving it.

Frank will meet the love of his life when he's barely out of school.

Frank will not know what's hit him when he meets his future wife. He won't be able to live up to her expectations, nor will he deserve her devotion.

Frank will never know love like he has for his children, and his home, and his German Shepherd Mick; for domesticity, although he'll fight it, in spite of himself.

Frank will not be able to stay faithful for more than a couple of years at a time, often much less, until he gets too old to think about that kind of nonsense.

Frank will find his love of caring for people when he takes a job transporting old and disabled people in his community bus. He will live in fear of ending his days like them.

Frank will not remember anything about any of these things for long periods of time, and when he does, and when he tries to say sorry for anything he's done wrong, it will be too little, too late.

Black, White and Red

If you put a gun to her head to ask her when she first lost her father, she would be a dead woman. She can't remember, is the truth. But she does know it happened when she was young enough to wear really short skirts and knee-high socks. And those red plastic sandals. They both had those – Dawn and her brother John. She remembers the feel of them, and the way they smelled. John hated them and would often moan to mum: 'Why do I have to wear the same shoes as Dawn?' But Dawn loved the way they connected her with her brother, and when they walked to school together she would narrow her vision down to the ground and watch their bright red plastic feet step left, right, left, right, like they were a two-man army and nothing, nothing, was going to separate them.

Back then, love seemed like a fleeting and mysterious thing. They saw it in Hollywood films starring ladies whose hairstyles were blonde and wavy, and who could get their be-hatted suitors to light their cigarettes. It was something their parents gave them, Dawn was sure, but they spent most of their time battling with and for each other. So having inanimate objects like sandals to love was something of a lifesaver.

There's a photo of her and John sitting on the steps that led up from the front garden of their council house to the street. An old black and white photo. From black and white days. Life's easier when everything has no shade, and is just one thing or the other. For them, then, the one thing was long, hot, summer school holidays, and the other was hearing their parents break up.

It became the soundtrack to their lives, like that series of albums called *Now That's What I Call Music*. Every track a classic hit: 'The Door Slammer'; 'The Flying Plates'; 'The Absent Father'; 'The Sobbing Mother'. All on side one of *Now That's What I Call Dysfunctional*.

In the black and white photo – the one that turned all the colourful drama into flat, monotone quiet – you can see their scuffed shoes and scraped knees. You can see the sheen of pretence. You can see their childhood innocence as they looked into the lens their mother pointed at them. Dawn knew it must be her mother because she – at least – was always there.

Wonky Stocking Seams

'Stand still, Liz, it's going wonky.'

Cynthia tried to keep a steady hand as she trailed the eyebrow pencil up the back of Liz's leg, but Liz was jigging around like someone plugged into the mains.

'I can't keep still, I'm too excited.' Liz reached for her Coca Cola and sucked on the straw she'd put into the neck of the bottle. She wished she had some rum in it, but her dad would knock her into next week if he smelled any booze on her. When she got in later, he'd be in bed with any luck, and he'd never know.

And she wouldn't risk him stopping her going out tonight. There was no way she was going to miss the night of the year at The Majestic. Jiving, and then live music; a new band of local lads called The Marauders. All of her crowd had been looking forward to it for ages. Cynthia said the lead singer was a dish. Looked like Tony Curtis, with the duck's arse hair at the back and the sexy coiffed curl at the front.

Liz wasn't bothered about all that. Not interested in boys. And it wasn't because her dad was a hard as nails Irish coal miner who would string a boy up by his nether regions if he so much as shook his greasy kiss curl at his daughter. She just wasn't interested in anything other than dancing.

'Courting's for fools,' she often told Cynthia, and Cynthia would always cluck her tongue and tell her one day she would fall and then she'd know it.

'Not yet, Cynth. Not me, not for a long time.'

*

They walked into The Majestic two numbers into The Marauders' set, with their fake pencilled stocking seams finally straight, and their new jive dresses crisp and swinging.

'God, see, Liz! Look, didn't I tell you he's a dish?' Cynthia nodded towards the stage.

Liz screwed up her face. She hadn't clocked him yet, but his voice was awful. There was no way she could ever fall for anyone who mangled Elvis Presley in quite that way.

No Way On God's Earth.

She looked towards the stage, towards the man whose voice sounded like a chicken being throttled.

She'd never seen hair that expertly coiffed, that Brylcreemed. Never seen eyes so intensely blue she could see them clearly even from twenty feet away.

Never felt her heart beat quite this rhythm before. Never fallen so fast.

'Christ, Cynth!' she gasped. 'Check the line on my nylons, will you?'

The Future

Her fingers were cold. He squeezed them tighter in his big palm; they were lost in there. It made him feel good. Her protector. Not that she needed protecting, from what he'd seen of her so far. Fierce, she was. When he told her he didn't dance she told him she would see her dance partner, Donald, twice a week, and when they were at The Majestic on Fridays and dancing non-stop, he wasn't to get jealous and start doing any of 'that macho nonsense'.

'Okay, Liz,' he'd said, incapable of any more words. Incapable of feeling anything except a thudding heart which meant the start of something, even though he didn't know what.

He took her to the café where everyone met before going to the dance halls. Choruses of 'Hey, Frank' and 'Frankie, my boy' and 'Frank, darling!', and Liz let it all happen; sat quietly, smoothing her skirt. Classy.

But when he came back with their coffees and put them down on the table, she let her hand cover his, stilling him for a second, and said:

'I mean it. I don't put up with nonsense.'

It was implicit that she meant the women who were batting their eyelashes, swooning over his film-star looks. The groupies who hung back after his gigs.

She made him want to be better. She saw past the dark shadow of his dad, the scars he'd etched in him. *You'll never be good enough* was now looking like it could be a lie. Was it?

Could he pull this off? This relationship thing? He could see the future stretching out before him like a never-ending ribbon of time and he wondered, for the first time, if he could navigate it and make it to the end, and be happy along the way.

Liz sipped her coffee, her pale blue eyes holding his gaze steadily. He knew she would always be the strongest of the two of them.

Making a Baby

Liz was a good Catholic girl. She'd never even dreamed of stuff like this.

She poured the pale green, apple-scented liquid into the running flow of the tap, leaned over and agitated it with her hand. The sharpness of Granny Smith filled her nostrils and made her feel a little dizzy.

She wasn't a virgin, they'd done stuff. But it had been hurried and furtive; some of it she didn't even think counted as sex. She'd got more semen on her stockings than inside her, and though the thought made her blush, she thought it was okay. She thought God might look the other way about stuff like that, because they were young and they were in love, and they didn't really know what they were doing.

But now, a gold band on her left hand changed everything. She was running a bath for her husband and they were going to get in it together.

She heard Frank in the bedroom next door; the jangle of his belt buckle as he undid it, the soft *flump* of his trousers on the floor, then a silence until the tinkle of his metal watch strap on the brand-new G-Plan dressing table. She heard him grunt faintly, and knew he was bending down to pull off his socks.

She removed her robe and stepped into the bath. As she sat, the bubbles tickled her intimately and she closed her eyes, savouring the feeling and the anticipation of her husband coming in to continue what the bath had started.

And then, he was there, in the doorway. The shock of his nakedness took her breath. Tanned from his garden work, lithe and lean with youth. She felt a lump in her throat; the love overwhelming.

The feeling was like a beautiful tune being played on a rare instrument, and it brought tears to her eyes. She didn't know if Frank heard the notes too, but his eyes were moist as he looked at her, and she could see his chest rising and falling; maybe he was breathing to the rhythm of that internal music.

'Hello, dear wife,' he said, and the newness of the title sent a delicious spasm through her.

'Hello, dear husband,' Liz replied, and she watched Frank step into the bath. She saw him more intimately than she'd ever done. He settled at the opposite end to her, taps at his back, and his legs snaked inside hers, his toes reaching, searching, probing...

She felt her skin prickle, goosebumps racing around every inch, even though the water was warm. A good Catholic girl. She was, she was! But she knew Frank wanted to do such wicked things to her. And she wanted it too.

And yet she knew God wouldn't be mad, because tonight, in hot green bubbles and with the soundless music in their hearts, they were going to make a baby.

That Rare 0.03%

The atmosphere on earth is made up of:

Nitrogen 78%. *Nitrogen is important for plant growth, and is present in the building blocks of protein in hair, muscles, skin, and other important tissues of the body. Nitrogen is a vital part of a human's diet and we get it in the form of protein.*

On the day his second child, Dawn was born, Frank waited in the corridor with a bunch of wilting daffodils, watching a cockroach crawl along the dirty skirting board and wondering how this had escaped the hospital cleaners. From the door to the room in which Liz was lying came a multitude of sounds: the kind-faced nurse cooing and coaxing, someone else saying 'Try not to push just yet', Liz's laboured breathing and occasional exclamations of pain. He felt guilty. He knew Liz had wanted him in there, even though the nurses had screwed up their faces about it. He'd told her: 'Best not to upset the applecart, love,' and had sighed with relief when she hadn't insisted. Going to get the flowers had been a distraction he'd welcomed. Golden yellow bunches spilled from bright red buckets outside the petrol station and he'd taken fifteen minutes to choose one; each minute a precious minute away from the madness. He'd picked up some chicken sandwiches too. The lettuce was as tired as the daffodils but there was no other choice. Liz would need something to build up her strength, and if she didn't want them, more for him.

When he finally got back to the hospital he felt bone tired, though he knew he'd done nothing to earn it. He sat on a metal chair with the daffs at his feet, half conscious until the sound of a new-born cry jolted him fully awake.

What he saw in the room stopped him in his tracks, stopped his tiredness. Stopped his heart. In a pink blanket lay a tiny, writhing body; red, with patches of a white waxy gunk. Masses of black hair. A girl, he saw, and his stomach gave a wrenching lurch like he was on a rollercoaster at Blackpool. A daughter. His life was never going to be the same again, because his one job from this moment was to protect her with every breath in his body. Only when those breaths stopped would that responsibility end.

Oxygen 21%. *Used in the medical industry e.g. for gas and air as anaesthetic.*

Frank joked that it was Liz's enthusiastic sucking on the gas and air pipe during labour that had determined Dawn's temperament. They must have got the mix of laughing gas and oxygen wrong, because you only had to look at Dawn and she would giggle in that gorgeous way babies had. Frank hoped it would never change, but it did, as she got older. And he knew that, mostly, it was his fault.

Argon – From the Greek word for lazy. 0.93%. *Uses Include: For treating heart arrythmias.*

Growing up, everything had been about sex.

Coming from a big family of girls and only one brother, Frank's education in that area had been watching his brother Harvey in the alleyway behind their house, with his hand up girls' skirts and his face stuck to theirs like he was trying to plunge a big poo out of a toilet. At night, in their bedroom, Harvey's bed across the room would often shake and Frank would hear muffled sounds like gasps and moans, and in the morning, Harvey would bundle up his sheets and sneak them into the laundry pile before their mum saw them. He knew it had something to do with girls because sometimes he'd hear Harvey moan the name of his latest girl. He wanted to ask him more, but he made do with watching him with this girl or that, learning from the master. And Harvey had a lot of time to cavort with girls, because all their sisters did all the housework. The two boys were allowed to be lazy. And to think, and talk, about girls and 'how's your father' pretty much all of the time.

When Frank met Liz, his heart started doing something weird. It wasn't so much about sex – well, maybe in the very beginning – but about emotions. He never thought he'd use that word. Never thought he'd look at a woman and have his heart race, or stop, or hurt, or swell, or any number of actual physical things. His heart beat a new rhythm and it was all because of Liz.

And when he first set eyes on Dawn, everything changed again. One minute he was one half of Liz and Frank, then he was one third of Frank, Liz and John (being dad to a boy was cool because he could show off his football skills and tell him stories you can't tell girls), and then suddenly he was a quarter of Frank, Liz, John and Dawn.

When he took Dawn in his arms for the first time, he held his breath and felt his heart stop beating, and didn't notice when it all restarted. She was perfect.

And now, everything was about love.

CO_2 0.04%. *Used in photosynthesis. Helps alleviate panic attacks*

Frank discovered that having a daughter meant he spent most of her early years removing hazardous materials and objects from the floor, and most of her teenage years twitching behind the curtain when she was dropped off after a date. He didn't know if this ever went away – this blind panic that he could never really protect her when it came down to it. And sometimes he didn't know if he had a right to worry when he was such a terrible father in so many ways.

But he carried on, and watching her unfurling like a brand-new leaf budding in spring was a joy he felt he could never get enough of.

Other 0.03%. *Helium and other trace gases.*

Dawn's rarity was what Frank loved the most. Her uniqueness. She was often quiet, preferring her own company to being in the thick of things, and he knew, just by looking at her, that she had so much going on inside her. She could grow up to be anything she wanted, he knew it. A doctor, a scientist, an astronaut. She could discover something amazing, cure diseases. Just the possibility of that made him proud, and the knowledge that she knew and believed it too.

Liz laughed at him when he told her, and in the end, Dawn didn't become or do any of those things. But she was kind, and caring, and creative. She was the most precious thing to him, floating around in the orbit of their family.

She was that rare 0.03% that danced around the atmosphere like musical notes too precious to commit to a tune. She would never be explained, nor tamed, nor fully understood by him. His beautiful enigma. His life.

His Dawn.

Whistle

You see flowers on the wall like a crooked line of bowing heads; yellow and orange and green, some split down the middle by a paper gap and a beige grey plaster scar. Some of the flowers seem close enough to touch, popping in front of you, jumping out in sharp relief.

You feel the warmth coming from his body, wrapped in the sheets beside you; hear the musical whistle of breath coming from his nose. Undulating sharp-pitch waves of a sound so familiar.

You hear that whistle when he's sitting in his armchair on Saturdays after *Match of the Day*, and Sundays after his chicken dinner. You hear it in church when he's supposed to be listening to Father Corrigan, and again when your mum is trying to tell him what so and so from up the road has been up to this week. And when it stops you get that wink from him like he's telling you that you have a secret with him. And you like it. It makes you laugh.

He moves now; a slow and lazy Sunday morning wake-up stretch, and you know it'll end soon... this weekly treat your mum allows, while she mops the floors and stokes the fire and makes the bread for later.

You lie in their bed and savour the warmth and peace of him while up the stairs drift the sounds of the house waking and the smell of the loaf baking.

And then the creaks and thumps of your brother, the yawn of your dad.

The call of your mum that breakfast is ready, marking the end of this magic.

I Just Can't Help Believing

Dawn gathered all her friends in the school yard at break time, with the promise she had something very exciting to tell them all. Sandra Smith had the usual look on her face that said nothing would impress her. Her dad was a vicar and she always told the kids at school that 'God was on their side', whatever that meant. Dawn reckoned that if her family were close friends with God, it probably meant that most things other people did seemed dull. God would make some pretty exciting things happen for a family if he was on their side. But today, Dawn had an amazing secret, and as far as she was concerned, it far outdid having a vicar for a dad and having God on standby.

'Well?' Sandra asked, visibly stifling a yawn. 'What's this exciting news?'

Dawn turned her head left and right, checking who was nearby. She leaned in towards the group: Sandra, Mary Wright, whose dad delivered coal, Antoinette Ducat, whose dad was apparently French but who no one had ever seen, and Jane Evans, as plain as her name. Her mum and dad ran the local paper shop.

'Elvis is coming to ours for tea,' she said, then opened her mouth in an excited but silent *WAH* and did a little 'jazz hands' wave.

'Wow! That's amazing!' said Antoinette.

'You're so lucky, that's brill!' said Jane.

'Oh my God!' said Mary.

Dawn felt a flush of pride. This was the best thing anyone had ever told anyone in the playground. Ever!

'What? When?' Sandra asked and then burst out laughing. 'Don't be stupid. He is not!'

This wasn't the reaction Dawn had expected, nor wanted, from Sandra Smith. She felt her face flush hot.

'He is! My dad invited him. He's coming Sunday at five o'clock. They're friends. From when my dad was in The Marauders.'

She could see this last bit of info had clearly rattled Sandra and stopped her just as she was about to say something else. It made perfect sense that her dad would know Elvis, because everyone in rock and roll knew each other, and her dad had sung lots of Elvis songs, which would have flattered The King no end and made him and her dad firm friends.

And, Dawn knew her dad wouldn't lie to her. He said Elvis was coming, and she believed him.

'Well, that's great,' Sandra eventually said, with a shrug of her shoulders, and then pretended this news was really boring as she inspected her nails. 'Tell us all about it on Monday.'

In Dawn's house, on Sunday, her mum fussed about the tea table more than usual, and about what they'd have to eat. Usually, after the formality of the tablecloth from lunchtime, they'd just have the mats on the bare table, and the usual fayre would be fish paste sandwiches, maybe a Bird's trifle or a tin of mandarin segments with evaporated milk for afters. But today, she'd made a Victoria sponge, and the sandwiches were tinned salmon and cucumber slices.

An excitement buzzed in the air. She and John were persuaded to have their baths early and to prepare their bags for school so they could stay up later and wouldn't have to fuss about it all in the morning. They both ran around like lunatics, throwing books and pens into bags, setting out their school clothes. Their mum and dad looked happy too, happier than for a long time. Dawn thought it must be really exciting for them too, because even though her dad had by all accounts been a good singer, he must be thrilled that someone as great and as famous as Elvis was coming to his house for tea.

It was the happiest the whole family had been for quite some time.

When five o'clock came and went, and stretched to six o'clock, then seven, Dawn asked her dad where Elvis was.

'He must have been delayed,' he answered. 'I gave him our phone number, but you know how famous people are. He doesn't really have to explain himself, does he?'

At first Dawn felt upset. What was she going to say on Monday? She was going to look like a fool and Sandra Smith would take the mickey out of her for certain. She wanted to believe her dad hadn't lied to her, that it had all been a mistake. Elvis just couldn't make it, right? But she couldn't help feeling sad.

But later, with everyone sitting around the table with their bellies full of salmon and two slices each of Victoria sponge, and with all chores done so that the evening stretched long and lazily in front of them, she watched her mum and dad laughing, holding hands, kissing, and felt that this evening had not been a disappointment at all.

Urban Love Affair –
The First Time

Forsaking All Others

You say it's a blokes' get together, but the lie stings your lips as it comes out of your mouth. You plan the hotel stay with fear and excitement in your chest. Both emotions are in equal measures delicious and terrifying. You can't stop thinking of her. She makes you forget all your vows. Makes 'until death' seem so long. You pack your clothes, feeling like a teenager. Feeling like the best and the worst human being all at once.

A Drink at the Midland Hotel

You both reach for the same glass by mistake; laugh. You feel cold condensation on your fingers, heat from hers. Outside, rain lashes down. Your room is warm and dry. As you take the lift you imagine the other people in it think you're married, and the thought pleases you. Your hand seeks hers secretly. You wish you were alone and can't wait for the lift to reach your floor. When it gets there, terror forms beads of sweat on your back. She notices the bloom of moisture and laughs, tells you she'll help you out of the shirt as soon as you get inside. The walk along the corridor to your room is the longest you've ever taken.

You don't think of Liz even once.

Deed
Lips that taste of whisky; a tongue of cigarettes and pleasure. Heat and friction. A pounding heart. A period of ecstasy too brief to matter, but it does.

You watch through the dressing table mirror the couple on the bed. They look beautiful and tanned and exhilarated; like movie stars. They look like they have no cares. The woman's red lipstick is smudged.

Leaving
In the cold light of day, you don't want to think about last night, but rain has turned Manchester's pavements into mirrors, and you see your shame reflected in every step. Outside the hotel, a clown with a red balloon is dancing for a crowd. His painted-on smile brings a flashback of her bright-red lipstick smeared on your face; a guilty, drunken mouth printed on your rough beard.

The End of Everything
On the way home, you drive most of the way in silence. You can't think of a single thing to say and you pretend you have a headache so she won't speak to you.

There's a dead bee on your dashboard. You weep at the sight of its legs frozen in time, and know it means everything is over.

Gypsy Toast

- A large frying pan, hot
- A spatula
- 2 whole eggs per person
- A splash of milk
- A whisk or a fork
- White lard – a lot
- Two slices of bread per person (white is best)

Dawn watched her dad as he stood in front of the cooker hob. He had a checked tea towel thrown over his shoulder and he was wearing the yellow flowery apron that was really her mum's. Dawn giggled because he looked really silly. Beside her, John clacked his knife and fork together like he was knitting, off in his own world as usual. Her mum drank a cup of tea with her eyes looking down at the tablecloth.

'Right, blossom.' Her dad dunked a big slice of Sunblest into the bowl and then lifted it and shook off the drips. He laid it in the frying pan and the kitchen became a sea of noise, loud hisses and sizzles; the chittering of a dozen chattering monkeys.

'Frank! The smoke!' Her mum was suddenly on her feet and doing her mad, wafting dance, waving a tea towel, dodging their German Shepherd Mick as he woofed and darted around her legs. 'John, get the door.'

Into the kitchen a breeze came, fresh as spring, along with the song of the birds and the creak of the rope swing on the giant oak at the top of the garden. Her mum gazed out, like her thoughts were escaping with the heavy black tendrils of smoke, and like she wanted to follow them. Dawn wanted to take her hand, shake it a bit, smile up at her. But she didn't. She'd do it later.

'Sauce bottle sentries at the ready!' her dad shouted as he flipped the bread over, and John lined up the red and brown sauce bottles, excitement animating his face.

Today's gypsy toast was golden, with dark and crispy eggy edges. Golden like the sun that cracked down between the oak's branches and painted their house with happiness.

Dawn liked this golden light when her dad was here a whole lot more than the heavy darkness when he wasn't.

The End

It was the end. It had to be. And yet... what was it they'd said, standing at the altar with both their families behind them, one on either side like on a battlefield?

Till death us do part.

People said it, didn't they, as if the promise will be easy to keep? Death seems so far away when you're twenty-two and just starting a life together. The 'in sickness' part makes you think of a bad hangover after a night on the razz, and 'for better or for worse' is going to be when the twin tub washing machine leaks, or the chicken gets burned on a Sunday.

You never think it's going to be anything bad, anything serious. You never think that all those vows and promises are meant to test the real strength of your relationship, like when jobs dry up and you wish you could even afford a twin tub washing machine or a chicken to burn.

They'd weathered all that. Redundancy, hand to mouth living, washing clothes in the bath, and eating bread and jam. The break-up of his 'band', if you could call it a band. Just old school friends messing about. There'd been some local success and lots of fans – mostly girls – but it had never really been serious.

Liz never thought for one moment that 'for better or for worse' was going to be about wondering when Frank was coming back from the pub, or whether he was going to smell of more than beer and cigarettes when he did. She didn't think it was going to be about lying awake at night and looking at him as he slept, wondering where he was in his dreams, and who with.

So when she found out, the shock was like a physical blow; as if someone had kicked her in the chest.

It had to be the end, didn't it?

She had no idea it was just the beginning.

Bus Notices (And What They Really Mean)

Seating Capacity: 132 (80 Seated, 52 Standing)

Their wedding was standing room only. Liz was amazed, and touched. Despite the ceremony being a full Catholic Mass – at the insistence of her father – people still came in droves.

It was amusing to see the pews filled with what her father called 'Edwardian throwback dandies' in their suits with velvet lapels, brothel creepers and greasy hair. And alongside them, all the old dears of the family in their fur coats and best hats, and the younger ones from her side in their sensible suits, dresses and shoes. Definitely squares compared to Frank's lot. It was like a mob of disparate people had been thrown together because of some natural disaster. Frank's family and hers. A mismatch if ever there was one.

Everyone Liz knew from work was there – all the lithographers, mould makers and kiln men. They scrubbed up really well, considering. Not a speck of pottery dust in sight.

And from Frank's job, the other drivers, conductors and conductresses.

Mostly conductresses.

Do Not Stand Forward of This Notice

Starting out in married life is never easy. You have to establish boundaries. Rules. You have to devote your time and attention to one person, and prioritise them over everyone else. *And forsaking all others....*

If someone thrusts themselves into your life un-invited and unannounced, it can only mean trouble.

And there was lots of trouble.

Please Do Not Distract the Driver

Liz could never understand why Frank married her – a woman with dark hair – if he appeared to have a thing for blondes. All the film stars he liked were blonde: Kim Novak, Jayne Mansfield, Marilyn.

The conductresses who distracted him. Always blonde.

Please Wait for the Bus to Come to a Complete Standstill before Alighting

Liz had never been a fan of scary stuff, rollercoasters and the like. Sometimes, Frank would try to persuade her on to the rides at Blackpool with the kids, but she always ended up being the one who waited with bags and coats until everyone came off giddy and squealing afterwards.

She'd tried it once, and had been sicker than she'd ever been in her life. John and Dawn had laughed so hard at her green face, while stuffing half a dozen donuts each into their own. She'd never lived it down.

But she hated feeling like she had no control. She wanted a quiet life. It took her a few years to realise she'd married the wrong man if she wanted quiet and still.

Please Place Used Tickets in the Bin Provided

If Frank had thrown away all his illicit receipts and tickets, hotel reservations, letters, notes, it might have taken her much longer to find out.

But he'd been careless.

No Smoking

Liz and Frank gave up smoking together and did really well. So she was surprised when she came home and discovered the smell of smoke. Frank said she was imagining it.

In Case of Emergency, Break Glass

If she hadn't been brought up a Catholic, maybe things would have been different. Divorce was not an option, and in God's eyes she would always be married.

Just a pity not in Frank's, apparently.

Sometimes – the times she found herself watching the clock hands move around in a quiet house when

John and Dawn were in bed and the past-midnight hours stretched long and lonely – Liz would try to imagine life without Frank.

Couldn't do it. Couldn't break the emergency glass. She'd said 'until death' and she meant it.

Not All Heroes Wear Capes

Today, Frank's showing Dawn and John how to be superheroes.

He'd caught John that morning, as he went to call him for breakfast, hiding under his blankets, and he could see a torch light shining under there. There was a circle like the Mysterons from Captain Scarlet penetrating through. He'd crept into the room slowly, stifling a laugh. Then he'd *bipped* John on the top of his head, eliciting giggles.

'What you reading, sport?' he'd asked, and John had made him sit for five minutes while he showed him what Superman was up to that week.

'You know you don't have to hide under the covers with a torch, don't you?' Frank asked. 'It's morning. It's light out.'

He'd pulled open the curtains, proving it.

'I know, Dad, but Superman likes danger. Do you like danger?'

Frank hadn't known how to answer that. He didn't *think* he liked danger, but for a while now, behind Liz's back, he'd been doing some pretty dangerous things.

Now, in the back garden with both John and Dawn, he fastens their matching anoraks using just the one top button. As he adjusts their hoods, his face is right up against theirs. Both have jam around their mouths. Both have the widest, bluest eyes. Both have snotty noses and hot breath, and he imagines their little hearts beating inside their chests. He closes his eyes and wants to hold on to this; this feeling that their hearts are all intact, even as he realises he'll probably break them both in two.

'Don't put your arms in. This is a superhero's cape,' he tells them, and his voice is thick.

'Where's yours, Daddy?' Dawn asks him, blinking the long eyelashes he'd first seen when she was seconds old. She'll never need fake lashes when she's older. He feels a cold hand clutch at his heart, compress his chest. It's like the draught from those batting lashes has knocked him over.

'I don't need one. Only superheroes need them. That's what you two are. You can do anything. You're both amazing.'

'But you *are* a superhero, Daddy.' Dawn smiles and finds his hand with her little one; sticky with something but he doesn't care. 'You're *our* hero.'

He wants to reply. He wants to tell them they shouldn't look up to a man like him. A weak man. But he doesn't, because being strong in their eyes is all he has left.

Waiting for the Slam

Parents are funny things, John thinks. They tell you not to lie, and then they lie through their back teeth at you whenever they get the chance. Double standards, his Aunt Mary would call it. She thinks everyone has double standards, and that everyone is out to 'do a number on her'. John knows it has something to do with the fact that Uncle Peter left one day to get some cigarettes at the off licence and no one's seen him since.

His mum lied that night he heard raised voices from their bedroom. He bumped into her on the landing when he was going to the loo and she was going downstairs for a glass of water. Her eyes were red and there were splodges of colour on her cheeks. 'I heard shouting. Are you okay, Mum?' John had asked and she lied to him, bold as brass. 'We were rehearsing a play,' she said, and John's stomach turned over. Not just because she'd lied, but because she was treating him like a baby. With a stupid story about a play! He was a big boy, and he always tried to tell the truth. Why couldn't parents be honest?

He used to watch his dad and wonder if he would bugger off one day when getting fags from the off licence. But he didn't. He left in broad daylight and didn't hide it. He came and kissed him and Dawn, hugged them fiercely, then took a suitcase and left.

Aunt Mary – who is his mum's sister, not his dad's – sat with his mum on the sofa for a few nights after that, poured vodka for her and told her it was only to be expected. He was a man and what else are they good for but chasing women and giving into their animal urges?

His mum agreed with her, and said, 'Never again! That bastard isn't welcome in this house.'

But that was another lie, because his dad came back, and the family watched him leave again later. And again, and again.

John doesn't trust his dad anymore. Whenever he's back, he watches him closely, looks for the suit-case, waits for the door to slam.

Heatwave

In the summer of '76 my cousin fried an egg on a car bonnet and had it for his tea. We watched with open mouths as he scraped it off with a spatula and strutted into the house for salt.

The air was suffocating. I walked barefoot outside and burned blisters into the soles of my feet that didn't heal for a month. At nighttime I watched the lightning streak across the tops of the roofs and felt the rumble of the thunder in my ears and my chest. When the thunder-rain came people rushed out of their houses and stood in it like they'd never seen rain.

It was a few weeks before I thought to wonder when Mum would call, like she promised. She never broke promises. Aunt Phyllis said Mum had her own storm going on.

*

My cousin Bridget and I played housewives. Our husbands were members of the Bay City Rollers.

Mine was Eric and hers was Woody. Neither of us liked Les, the lead singer, but he often came to our pretend houses to visit his bandmates for pretend tea and biscuits. Sometimes the tea and biscuits were real, but our marriages weren't, and I often wondered if the best marriages were real or pretend, and how on earth you'd know the difference.

'How long are you staying, Dawn?' Bridget asked, and I didn't know so I told her three months. Her smile widened, because in her crazy house with thirteen kids, I think she liked that I was quiet.

*

I had to be quiet in my house, silently tiptoeing around my parents and the noise that often came from their bedroom.

It sounded like whimpering; that thing puppies do when they're scratching at the door to be let out, or sitting beside your chair at the dining table begging for scraps. I always put my hands over my ears: *La la la*. Willing it away.

When it did stop, it was a scary stop, and from my room I'd put my head to the wall to listen. My ears would penetrate through daisy wallpaper, through brick and dust, through teal-with-gold-fleck paper, across prickly air to the mouth of my father.

'Stop nagging,' that stern mouth often said, and I'd imagine the neatly combed hairs of his moustache quivering with the seething control of his words. I hated when they had fights. It happened far too often. Then dad would leave and my world always crashed down.

*

On another sultry day, The Bay City Rollers were having a press conference in Bridget's bedroom. We had the windows open and a million tiny flies had swarmed in.

I was flicking some off my arm when Phyllis shouted upstairs that mum was on the phone. I walked down the stairs with shaky legs.

Praying he hadn't gone. Not again.

Affairs of the Heart

Frank tore off tiny bits of toilet paper and stuck them on his face. Scarlet flowers bloomed in the white and he winced at the sting. Shaving was never normally this bloody, but today, he couldn't keep his hands from shaking.

Mick was waiting for him in the kitchen, his head in his paws. Looking out of the window, Frank saw what Mick's huge brown eyes were telling him; that it was a gorgeous morning with that rare golden light it was a joy to walk in. But he didn't know if he could do it. He didn't know if his legs would be strong enough to get them further than the garden gate.

'In a while, old mate,' he said, and at the sound of his voice, Mick's tail thumped the floor, but his face looked quizzical. Mick's love for him was unconditional and he was the most obedient dog. But today, Frank didn't doubt that the sound of his wavering voice – an octave or two higher – was causing some confusion.

From above his head, in the bedroom over the kitchen, he could hear sounds of Liz stirring. In about ten minutes she would be downstairs, making tea, talking about so and so and what they were up to, boiling eggs. Then the kids would be getting up.

Frank didn't want tea, and he didn't want egg and soldiers. His stomach was reeling like a drunken Irish dancer, and if he ate or drank anything this morning, he'd probably be painting the wall with it two minutes later. And he couldn't face the kids. Not yet.

He had to tell Liz first, and hopefully he'd be able to pack and gather all his things together before John and Dawn got up.

He heard her feet on the stairs and lit a cigarette to steady his nerves.

A Decision Has to be Made

There comes a time in everyone's life when they have to ask a really simple question: *Do I do what's right and face the consequences, or do I leave well alone and forget I ever knew anything?*

Liz's hand hovered over the bell. She noticed her nail varnish was chipped and thought: *I bet hers never is. I bet she has perfect crimson talons and perfectly straight stockings, not a hair out of place.*

Cynthia had told Liz what she looked like, this woman. She'd seen her with Frank at the bus drivers' café in the bus station. She was a conductress apparently. Pretty and blonde. 'Vacuous though,' Cynthia added, loyally.

Liz had asked if she was sure there was something going on because, if she worked on the buses too, she was entitled to be in the café, even to be sharing a cup of tea and a laugh with Frank.

'Well, yes, Liz, she would be entitled to that,' Cynthia said. 'I've seen Frank do that with his male workmates before. You have too. But I've never seen him sitting thigh to thigh with them, pushing their hair off their face, and whispering into their ear until they're giggling like schoolgirls.'

'Bloody hell, no!' Liz shook her head. 'That would be a whole other pickle we'd be in if that were the case!'

She laughed, but the humour only served to highlight how unfunny this was.

Another one. It was happening again. He swore last time he'd never do it again, but he was doing it.

'I've seen them in the pub too, Liz. I'm sorry.'

Frank never suspected she was following him. He said he had an extra shift, and took his bag and everything, but he'd showered for the second time that day and worn his best underpants. Cynthia, who'd been on stand by for this for weeks, was waiting around the corner in her old man's car for Liz, and they trailed him keeping a discreet distance.

As Liz walked up to the front door, she tried to imagine the kind of woman who'd sleep with a man she knew had a wife and two young children. There could be no denying she knew – she was a work colleague. When she looked in the mirror to fluff up her blonde hair and apply her scarlet lipstick, did she like what she saw? Could she look herself in the eyes?

Liz knew if she rang the bell now, there'd be no going back. She'd be forcing Frank to make a choice. And she'd have to make one too. She'd have to decide whether to forgive him or not.

Her finger hovered over the bell, and she closed her eyes and silently asked God to help her make the right choice.

Gone

The typewriter had been in the hall, by the front door, all morning. On running downstairs, into the kitchen to get their Ready Brek, and back out to the living room to stick on the cartoons, Dawn and John almost fell over it three times each.

From the sink, elbow deep in suds, their mum called out 'Be careful' every time, each shout getting louder, shriller. Dawn thought she sounded funny.

The trip hazard sat motionless, a puzzle to be solved. Every time she tiptoed past, Dawn eyed it curiously, wishing it could speak to her. It was her father's most treasured possession, on which he wrote his 'Letters to the Editor' that often appeared in their local *Sentinel* newspaper. It always lived in the safety of his wardrobe when not being used. And though it was rich in vowels and consonants, it remained devoid of words to explain itself today.

Bugs Bunny and Yosemite Sam didn't hold Dawn's attention this morning. She stirred her Ready Brek round and round until it was cold and gluey, listening to John giggling, and also to the sound of her mum in the kitchen, rattling dishes alone until the low hum of her dad's voice took over.

Dawn crept into the hallway and held her breath outside the door to the kitchen. She couldn't really hear what they were talking about, but she did catch the occasional 'Good boy. You're a good boy'; and little doggy yips from Mick. Her dad's voice sounded like being a good boy was a very sad thing.

The typewriter looked up at her, driving her mad with the secret she knew it was keeping by being in the way. What did it all mean? Sunlight from the front door panel highlighted the left side – the letters Q W E R / A S D F / Z X C V – and Dawn made words in her head from the letters, thinking this could be a code. Draw. Read. Fear. This last made her shudder, because the stifled tears of her mother, the occasional whimpering from Mick, and the sad tone of her dad's voice did fill her with fear.

She heard someone approach the door and she ran back into the living room before she was caught. When her dad came in, she stuck a spoonful of cold Ready Brek into her mouth. It tasted vile, felt claggy, but she tried to swallow it down.

'Hey, blossom.' He approached her, ruffling John's hair on the way. John was watching Bugs pull a giant carrot out of a really small hole in the ground, and was laughing like a maniac. 'How's my girl?'

She couldn't speak, using the chewy Ready Brek as an excuse to stay mute. He sat next to her on the sofa and she bounced up and down with his weight. He smelled of the Brut he always used from the dark green bottle in the bathroom cabinet, but under it, something not quite nice was being covered, like he'd been out all night and hadn't washed.

'I love you, blossom,' he said, and Dawn smiled and said, 'I know. I love you too, Daddy.'

And then, though she didn't know why, he started to cry, although he didn't make any noise like she and John, or her mum always did. He just wiped the quiet tears off his cheeks, stood up and left the room.

Dawn watched him pick up a bag, then the typewriter, and leave through the front door, leaving an empty space in the block of sunlight that had lit up the keys. She thought of more words... Fade, sad, scared, scar.

And more words – an incomplete 'DAD', an incomplete 'DAWN'.

Hairy, Tickling Toes

Our Dawn could never walk past dad without touching him: his knees, his forearm, the tip of his foot that rested across the opposite side's knee. Inside the slippers we'd seen mum pick out at British Home Stores, we knew he had big, hairy toes. Sometimes he would torment Dawn with them – the unslippered and unsocked version of them – and make them snake over her legs as they sat at opposite ends of the sofa; he'd make them tickle her belly until she screamed for mercy. She'd beg me to help – *John! John!* – but I knew she didn't really need her big brother. She loved it. She loved him beyond anything.

Before bed she'd sit on his knee and watch the telly, thumb of one hand in her mouth and the index finger of the other one twirling her hair as her eyelids unrolled like shutters to close her down for sleep. Her heart would lie against his chest – I imagined two beats of hers for every one of his. And I'd envy that closeness she had to him. The closeness that used to be mine before she came.

When mum woke us that strange morning, the house was quiet apart from the faint hum of cartoons in the living room and the clack of spoons on bowls as Dawn and I sat before it eating cereal. No arguing. No fighting. No shouting.

Dad's mug was still in the drainer from tea last night. His slippers were still by the fire, without his feet in them.

And his best coat was gone.

We waited for three weeks for him to come and put his slippers on and to hang his coat back on the hook. And during those weeks we ate all our meals in silence and mum would always have a glass of funny smelling water with hers.

When at last he did come back, we both wanted to run up to him and throw our arms around his neck, but mum made us go and play in our rooms, out of the way. So we went upstairs, and Dawn and I lay on the floor in my room which was above the living room, our ears against the carpet, listening to his muffled voice. I pictured his hairy, tickling toes warm again at last, and that night I let Dawn throw her arms around my neck instead.

His Lover

Frank wakes with his face in his lover's hair. She has it draped across both their pillows. It's long, and the morning light breaking through a gap in the curtains has caught in it and turned it into spun gold. On the bedside table are the pins that hold it in the tight bun she wears at work, and he remembers pulling them out one by one last night.

'Mm, your hair smells like apples,' he says, and for a second his insides clench around a memory; his first bath with his wife, with their limbs entangled in pale green, apple-scented bubbles. He wants to blank it out.

His lover makes him breakfast, but he barely touches it. He doesn't like the quiet of her house. He doesn't like the empty space in her kitchen where the dog bed should be. He doesn't like that her telly is not playing cartoons constantly on a loop, and that there isn't a line of muddy shoes by the front door.

He gives his lover a lift to work, which is also *his* work. It's risky, but he drops her around the corner and she walks the few yards alone while he parks his car.

In the canteen, over brews, he hears his lover's girlfriends ribbing her because they spotted her getting out of his car, despite their cautiousness.

"What did you get up to last night, you dirty mare?" one of them asks and the comments are relentless and ribald.

He asks one of his mates for an alibi for last night, and tells him where he really was. His mate winks. Says: 'Say no more.' Taps the side of his nose.

His lover asks him to give her a lift home. He doesn't want to because he wants to go home and be there when John and Dawn come home from school. Dawn has been working on a project about the Tudors and he wants to see what mark she got, and John was going to make a rocket or something. He's mad with himself that he doesn't remember.

But he says yes and takes her, and when she tries to kiss him before getting out of the car, he turns his head away.

'What's the matter, Frank?' she asks.

'I forgot what he's making in woodwork.'

'Who?'

'John, I forgot what he's making.' Now he feels tears starting.

'So,' his lover says. 'Does it matter?'

He leans across her and opens her door.

'Of course it matters,' he says, and starts the engine, wanting her out.

Innings

Out in the churchyard, John laid the petals on Dawn's eyelids, leaned over, lips against her ear.

'Ssshh. Don't move or speak,' he whispered. 'Let's just think of Ganga.'

From the road the sound of cars swishing past the church. They sounded like the hangers in his mother's wardrobe yesterday when she'd been looking for something to wear for the funeral. Her fingers had frogmarched over frigid, dark-coloured dresses, resting on each one impatiently for just a second before flicking it away along the rail. He guessed she was irritated because their dad had been acting weirdly all morning. One minute as quiet as a mouse, one minute shouting about things he wouldn't normally care about – like shoes in the way or Lego on the living room carpet – and the next minute sitting in his armchair with his head in his hands. John knew he'd never really got along with Ganga.

'Do you think Ganga can see, John?' Dawn asked, and John thought of those pennies, laid on his grandfather's eyes, his tiny body lost among the coffin's white silk and his too large grey suit and white shirt. Their mum hadn't wanted them to see the body, but their dad had said it was life, and reality, and sometimes truth was ugly. John didn't think Ganga had looked ugly. He'd looked like he was asleep, like he'd wake up any moment and shout 'Boo!' like he did in the games they played.

'I said don't speak,' John scolded. He lay down beside her; placed petals on his own eyes. He smelled the faint rose scent and thought of the bottles on his grandmother's dressing table, next to the framed photo of Jesus showing his heart. Bottles so pretty, with diamond shapes cut into them that always caught the sunlight and danced on the wall, and squeezy balloon things that fitted in his palm and puffed out the scent.

Ganga had some bottles on there too, but his were not so pretty. Square, straight, flat or fat, with man's colours. A man's scents. He always smelled of woodchips, tobacco and sweet toffee. John wondered if his grandmother would keep his bottles on the dressing table now Ganga was gone, and hoped she would, because he'd be able to smell them and bring Ganga back in his mind.

Everyone kept saying he'd had a good innings. He wasn't sure what that meant, but it made John think of being cuddled in his arms, face buried in his cardigan, his nose filled with the smell of wood and wool. Maybe an innings was a way of holding someone in your arms, and making them feel safe and loved, and very happy.

'Are we going soon, John? We will be late for the church.'

'In a minute.' John pulled his scarf up around his mouth and nose, filling his senses with wool and memories.

The Man of the House

When John hides in the basement underneath the kitchen and living room, everything changes. Everything becomes noise, nothing else, and this changes his world.

His mum sounds happy and light-footed. He can hear her dragging the Hoover around the lounge, shoving furniture out of the way; that table his dad made out of an old Singer sewing machine treadle. He stuck a bit of old oak on top of it. His mum never liked it and she always pulls a face and growls, like their dog Mick growling at a postman, when she moves it, but John can't see that. He just hears the Hoover, singing its high-pitched song, and hears his mum's feet clomping around doing the housework like she's dancing an Irish jig.

When his dad left his mum – the last time, not all the times before that – it was the school holidays and Mr Wilson from next door was mowing his lawn with one of those petrol things you have to pull the string on about fifty times before it sparks into life. It was making a hell of a racket while John and his sister Dawn were playing hangman and they'd had to shout:

'F!'

'NO, NOT F!' and John scratched the crossbeam of the gallows on the paper. His felt pen squeaked loudly as if it were trying to get a word in.

'I said 'S'!' shouted Dawn.

'NO S!' and John scratched another line, ready for the noose.

Their parents had the living room door closed but they could hear their raised voices, as if they were both trying to shout above the noise from Mr Wilson. Cupboards banged and china rattled, and then the jingle of their dad's keys and the swish of his coat as he shot along the hallway. The lawnmower got louder for just a second and then the SLAM of the door, the glass rattling.

Sometimes, after he and his sister are in bed, pink and steaming hot from their baths, John hears his mum open the cabinet in the living room where he knows she keeps the vodka. She's not supposed to drink because of something to do with her liver, but he can hear the fizz of the Schweppes and the plink of the ice cubes, and later – often not much later – the deep rumble of her snores.

Down in the basement is John's own little world. No one comes. They all go about their life above and he hears it all like it's a film or a play on the radio; not real. He can block it all out; the fights he hears, the sobs and the slamming doors.

Sometimes he imagines he's in a Wild West adventure, sitting backwards on an old deckchair, beating at the side of it with a fly swatter, shouting: 'Come on, hoss, we have to get to Dodge to shoot the bad guys. Yeeeee haaaaw.'

And that makes him feel good. Big and brave; the man of the house. One of the times his dad left, his mum told him that's what he was now, and that he was a good boy – so good.

He thinks that tomorrow, he'll bring Dawn down here. He could drag the other deckchair out of the corner and let her sit on it; she could be a female bounty hunter. Maybe bring some pop and sandwiches down, or some left-over supper. Heinz Beans with pork sausages! That would be better for cowboys. And a flask of coffee, like they drink in the Wild West out of tin cups.

And afterwards he'll help his mum make their tea and get lunches ready for school. He'll watch *Coronation Street* with her and try to take her mind off things and maybe stop her from drinking the vodka.

Being the man of the house is a big responsibility.

Mondays Without Mick

Every Monday; that dreaded day.

The shiny wet liver that almost seemed to pulse with the blood of the creature that lost it. Tubes, tough like rubber piping, sinews that stuck in our teeth.

Our mother always seemed able to suck every drop of moisture from that organ, rendering it far from vital. Then she would throw the moisture back on top of it in the form of thick and gloopy gravy, fat and glistening with onion pieces that looked like the shelled wings of cockroaches.

Our father would distract her attention, allowing us to slyly drop chunks of the dry offal under the table and into Mick's jaws. Often, later, we would find around the house sad, regurgitated pieces in the most ridiculous places; dad's slippers, the newspaper rack, once in mum's open handbag.

When Mick died, Mondays became a hell of a lot trickier. Organ offloading is no longer an option and we sit, as a family, and silently mourn the passing of our dog.

Items in an Adulterer's Holdall

Toiletries:
- For hair: Brylcreem, comb, shampoo.
- For moustache: Small comb, mascara. Frank doesn't want to admit it to anyone, but grey hairs have started to appear. When he first noticed them, he'd been in the bathroom shaving, and Liz's mascara had been sitting on the side where she'd left it that morning. A couple of flicks with the wand later, and the problem was gone. So Liz's mascara had 'mysteriously' gone missing and no, Frank didn't know where it was, and she ought to take more care of where she left things.
- Soap in drawstring bag. A soap-on-a-rope his daughter Dawn had got him for Christmas last year. It's a unicorn, but the horn has worn away. It's a bit of a joke, because she's twenty, but it's a throwback to when she was little and obsessed with unicorns. Frank doesn't care if it's ironic or not, and doesn't

even care that it smells like roses. He'll keep on using it until all there's left is rope.

- **Brut aftershave.** A classic, in the green bottle with the long neck, with a little tin plaque like a medal hanging around it. When his boy John was six or seven, he'd always pull them off and give them to his teddies or action men as awards for bravery. Frank wonders if John lets his own son do that. Makes a note to ask him.
- **Face flannel.**

Clothes:
- **Slacks.** Frank doesn't do jeans anymore. The only jeans he's ever worn are drainpipes, but since he hit forty, those days are over. He likes the comfort of slacks, even though he knows they are kind of square. He always gets Liz to iron out the creases and scrunches them up a bit so they look cooler.
- **Three shirts (one for travelling there, one for the evening, one for travelling back).** It takes him half an hour to choose his shirt for the evening. He eventually decides on his black silk one, because he's been told he looks sexy in it. He hides it at the bottom, underneath the others, just in case.
- **Trainers for driving.**
- **Black leather boots.** To wear with his black silk shirt.

- Three pairs of underpants (two blue y-fronts, one navy boxer). He puts the boxers underneath the black silk shirt.
- Socks.
- Jacket.

For the journey:
- **Sweets.** Opal Fruits and barley sugars. He won't be on the road long, but any excuse to eat sweets.
- **Don Williams cassette.** Because the soul of a country boy lies beneath his rock 'n' roll heart.
- **A to Z map book.** He's never been where he's going before. He's afraid of getting lost. He's more afraid he already is.

For hotel:
- **Print out of booking.**
- **Cash for drinks.** How much is rose wine, he wonders.
- **Condoms.** He pushes those all the way into the toe of his black leather boots.

Deceipt/Receit

The constant static crackle was annoying. Liz slammed the oven shut, sending an intense burst of hot roast chicken smell into the air. Across the kitchen, at the table she'd need to set soon, Frank was slouched in his chair; head back, gaze focused on nothing, listening intently to his CB radio.

CQ, CQ, CQ, the radio suddenly implored. A faint voice with an accent. Frank sat upright.

'Here he is,' he said. Not to Liz, who was loudly stirring gravy, but to himself. 'Marlon. From Florida!'

Liz clattered the spoon on to the side. 'Fucking Marlon!' she muttered. She wished she was in Florida, because apparently that's where she needed to be to speak to her husband.

'Can't you turn that thing off?' she asked. 'Dinner's almost ready.'

'But it's Marlon.' Frank reached out and twiddled the knob, increasing the volume of the voice and the crackling. 'I need to speak to him.'

'You need to speak to *me*, Frank. I need to speak to *you*.'

She took the receipt from the cutlery drawer where she'd hidden it earlier. A bar bill from a hotel in town, from the night Frank had been on his CB radio get-together with all the friends she'd never met.

Not the friends from Florida, but the friends who lived right under her nose.

She unfolded the receipt, smoothed it out.

One beer, one rose wine. She couldn't believe it was happening again. She thought all that nonsense was behind them.

'Turn it off, Frank, I'm serious. We really need to talk.'

Searching

This wheel is supposed to do something significant. Frank knows this. He knows that if he does things in a certain order, the car will move forward. But he doesn't know what those things are, or what the order is. So he grips the wheel and closes his eyes, searching inside his head for any clues that might be lurking behind the fractured clutter in there.

Something glints in his memory's eye – metallic, like light is bouncing off it. A key. Dangling.

The first key he'd owned had been to a council house he and Liz had moved into the week after their wedding. He'd carried her over the threshold like you're supposed to, breathing in the smell of her hair as she had clung to his neck. Feeling the warmth and softness of her cheek next to his. Hearing her laughter and squeals and feeling the delicious weight of it all on his heart.

It was the key he'd used to open the door when bringing their two children, John and Dawn, back from the hospital, one by one, to fill their home.

Ah, yes! A key. He has to put that in somewhere. Somewhere around this... steering column? Below the wheel. Yes.

He opens his eyes again; the glinting metal shrinks behind the clutter, its light out.

He doesn't even think to wonder lately where his wife went. Where his life went. He lives in a strange house with a strange woman, and the two young ones who visit remind him of someone, something, some place...

He knows, he knows, that he has to do some things in a certain order and if he does, the car will move forward. But he doesn't know what those things are, or what the order is. He grips the wheel, closes his eyes. Searches.

Time Bomb

'How on earth did we end up here?'

Frank's fingers gripped the wheel so hard his knuckles were white. The tick of the engine sounded like the signal that a bomb would soon go off.

He didn't know the answer, so said nothing. Beside him, Liz was fuming as she repeated the question.

'I don't know, Liz,' he said finally. He felt a dull pain starting to bloom in his temples. It had started just outside Tamworth, when they'd still been on the right road.

'I think… I think the… the computer map-display thing confused me.'

'The what?'

'You know…' He could still hear the strange noise in his head, the awful whooshing noise whenever a big lorry rattled past. The drivers were like kings up there in their cabs, looking down on him. It made him feel vulnerable, weak; every one of his seventy-five years. Back in his days as a long-distance lorry driver, he used to love looking down on the people in cars, feeling like he ruled the motorway. His right arm out of the window and the sun turning it nut brown. Those were the days he was invincible, a man earning money and bringing it home to his family. His wife and two kids. Was it two? Or three?

'You mean the satnav? How can the satnav confuse you? It tells you exactly where to go, where to turn off. And besides, why do you need a satnav in the first place? You can drive the length and breadth of the UK blindfolded.'

Frank's temples throbbed. He looked over at the woman sitting next to him. Had he brought a passenger with him? She looked angry and he felt certain it was with him, like he'd done something wrong.

'I told you to turn off at Junction 15,' she said. He turned the words over for a minute or two in his head. Junction 15. Junction 15. What did that mean?

'Oh, you're hopeless,' the woman – Liz, Liz, yes, his Liz – said. 'Junction 15 was ages ago and now we're in bloody Liverpool!'

'Oh, Liverpool!' Frank grinned. 'Remember when we went to see the Beatles at the Cavern Club?'

'That was years ago, Frank.'

'No, no. Not that long ago. You looked so pretty. That dress you thought was too short, but I loved it because you've great legs, Liz.'

She did have great legs. When the Fifties moved into the Sixties he'd thanked the Lord, because she'd ditched her jiving dresses for minis, and her nyloned legs for bare flesh. That was a lot to be thankful for.

'Shall we check if the Beatles are playing the Cavern while we're here?' he asked. 'Your mum won't mind having the kids for a while longer.'

Funeral

In the lid of the coffin that's Liz's heart, nails have been firmly hammered. The funeral hasn't even been arranged yet, but its accoutrements have been ordered in her mind.

Frank once made a TV unit out of a slab of rich, nutty mahogany he'd found at an old house clearance from the home of a deceased carpenter. It had the markings of something once destined for greatness, but which had never reached its potential. Frank said it deserved to do something noble, so he sawed it into five parts, and it lived out its life as the furniture which held the most important thing in the house.

So, his coffin will be made of mahogany.

On its lid she'll lay a cross of flowers. Frank's not religious, but she is, and she doesn't want to risk the wrath of God. She watches Frank now. He's in the garden and she's in the laundry room; he's out on the damp lawn, standing at the flower border, deadheading his favourite red roses. His hands are shaking as he tends the blooms, and she remembers how they'd shaken when he'd placed her wedding ring on. He'd been skinny as a whippet back then, and hadn't eaten for two days before the wedding. She'd grabbed his hand, just for a second. Squeezed it. Wanted the gesture to say, *It's okay. When you can't be strong, I can.*

She wishes she could be strong now. She needs to focus. She thinks of what he can wear to his final resting place.

She takes a few shirts from the dirty laundry basket and holds them up one by one. None of these is really suitable. They all smell of Lynx Africa and fear. For the past six years fear has been seeping from his skin, gathering in the fibres of his clothes, and lying dormant there, waiting for the shrinking of his brain to make all his fear go away.

A bee lands right in the middle of the biggest rose in the bush, and Frank leans towards it and coaxes it on to his finger. He looks over at the house and catches Liz's eye. All that love from a fifty-five-year marriage travelling across the garden of their final home together. He lifts his finger in the air and smiles the biggest smile, and she wonders, how long will that smile stay?

She puts his dirty shirts into the washing machine. She'll keep washing them until it's time for someone else to.

88

Progressive Regression

It's like someone has put a piece of gauze in front of my face. Everyone seems blurred, faded, out of reach. I hear voices but I can't make out words. Maybe the odd one, like 'Dad' and 'Love' and 'Remember?', but I don't, that's the point. I don't remember.

And yet sometimes I do. I remember holding my babies for the first time and smelling them. The good smells, like the flesh on top of their heads, and the bad ones like the ones that came from their backsides when they needed changing. And I changed them, even though it wasn't really the thing for a man to do it. I did it willingly, happily.

No one asks if I remember that.

And I remember my Liz walking down the aisle in the white dress with the flouncy skirt, and the look on her face that said she was going to do me some mischief tonight, and the way my heart exploded in my chest whenever our eyes would catch over the shoulder of someone else, someone who wasn't in on our secret.

Why doesn't anyone ask me if I remember our secret?

Then I'm back to forgetting and everyone is getting annoyed at me and saying they're sick of repeating themselves, and telling me to stop asking the same thing over and over, and I want to tell them I can't help it, but the words float out silently from my open mouth and drift past them while they stand looking at me as if I'm something incredible, something alien. I see their faces contort like they want to smile at me, but something big and scary they swallowed down is threatening to come up, and it twists their faces into something that's a hybrid of anger and grief.

Then... another memory, of long road trips, sometimes in a work van and sometimes with my love beside me and my other two loves behind me, singing and playing I Spy, and chanting 'Are we there yet' over and over. The adventure of it, the sheer joy, driving through Big Sky Country and watching fork lightning zap the road ahead, the future we were yet to reach.

Further back, memories of Him, the one who frightened us when we were little. The one with the booming voice who was gone a long time, being a soldier, and then came back to wreak upon his family the damage that had been done to his mind and the pit of his soul. And we took it, all that shit he doled out. We lived it, and then we all escaped it one by one.

When I look in the mirror now I see him, his face melded with mine, and the eyes that look out are blue in colour and mood, and are him, and then they're not. It all fades, and I feel a faint ticking inside my chest that's just marking time.

When I speak, no one hears me, no one understands. So I shout *No!* and kick doors and thrash my arms and sometimes they hit the woman who looks like Liz but older, without the flouncy skirt or the look on her face that says she'll do me some mischief. I want to tell this woman I'll pay her anything, give her anything if she can make my voice work properly and if she can bring back the babies so I can sniff their heads and their backsides. But the babies whose nappies I changed are bigger and more beautiful but further away now.

They're distant like unattainable, unrequited love.

Fly Away

In his head were all manner of fantastical ideas and he drew them, daily and manically, on the walls, the doors, the windows with permanent marker. He wanted Liz to see the visions he had, to make her understand the urgency. If they didn't go now, it would be too late.

But she just shouted at him: 'Frank! What on earth are you doing?' over and over until the sound of it, and the pressure of it, hurt his head.

Yesterday, she'd even tried to scrub off the ones on the windows because, she said, the neighbours would think they'd lost their marbles.

'Why permanent marker, Frank?' Her voice shook with anger, or the motion of her scrubbing, or both. Frank thought she would put the window through.

'Here, Liz,' he'd said, grabbing her hand and pulling her over to the chimney breast, where the majority of his diagrams and drawings were scrawled. 'These are the main ones, the main designs. I think this one, with the large double wings, will be enough to lift us.'

It had caused Liz to throw the dirty, wet rag at him and storm out, so he sat on the floor for a while, with his head down on his knees, thinking how on earth he could get her to see.

When he'd met her, she'd been the strong one. There was no doubt about that. Like all women, battling through a world that was all for men when you really looked at it. But she weathered it, and bore two children, and endured so much.

He'd put her through so much.

But now, he had a chance to put it right. These drawings and diagrams were the blueprints of the machine that was going to fly them out of here. He felt the danger. Felt it in his head, at the very core of him. Something was trying to eat him alive, with needle sharp teeth eating into his brain. Like a wolf feasting on a lamb.

It would only be a matter of time before it came for Liz. He had to build the machine as soon as possible so they could fly away. He couldn't take her away through the front door and in the car, because he didn't recognise anywhere out there now, and he couldn't figure out how to start the car.

But he had to get her away, because it was the only way he could hold on to her, and all the things they'd shared over fifty-five years.

He heard someone come back into the room while his head was still in his lap. He felt a cool wisp of air as they sat down next to him.

'I'm sorry, Frank.'

He felt the warmth of a hand on his cheek, lifting his face, his head, until he was looking into eyes so blue they were triggering something, some memory he could barely grasp.

'Where's Liz?' he asked. 'I need to fly her away from here.'

Two Heartbeats

You hold your breath, count your heartbeats, walk through memories that feel like a swamp, with something lurking beneath ready to take your legs from under you. He's sitting in a chair and the sight of him leaves you broken. Gossamer wisps of fine grey hair are caught in the filigree of the crocheted antimacassar. You remember the ones your nan had on her chairs and how you and the much younger version of him would laugh because they were for old people and you were five and he was twenty-eight, and every time your nan straightened them he'd pull faces at you behind her back, and your stomach would roll with mirth and joy and fear of her catching you.

You never expected him to get old. You lived with him in perpetual youth through your shared love of the ridiculous, but you don't see anything funny now.

You miss his laugh; raucous and joyful as a child's. His stupid pranks. That camouflage hat he used to joke made him invisible.

He'll never be invisible to you. You watch as the sun shines through the window into the lounge and bathes him in warm orange light. Everyone around him pales. All sound fades.

And you forgive him, like a good daughter would.

You sit beside him, take his hand. It's hot and his pulse is throbbing strong in your palm, matching your own beat. You close your eyes and you're a baby again, and he's a child-father, and you're lying naked on his chest, your heartbeats synced.

He Needs Nothing

He used to need women, alcohol, food, compliments, excitement. He needed to hear how fabulous he was, how handsome, witty, charming.

He needed his kids to love him and his wife to adore him. To forgive him.

Now he needs to be showered and shaved, to have his finger and toenails clipped, his beard trimmed and his ears and eyebrows de-fuzzed.

His arse wiped.

His food pureed.

His bedside fitted with a fall mat.

He needs his past life framed and hung on his wall so he can stand and stare at it like it belongs to someone else.

All his needs are met, but he needs nothing.

A Dipping Cuppa

As kids we huddled around the breakfast bar in our parents' mortgaged-to-the-hilt modern semi (*Brunswick Homes – where your dreams are made*), sat like the three wise monkeys, waiting for the toast.

Dad would be on buttering duty. Mum would pile the slices and he'd knock that pile down, slathering the marge on them one by one. Thick gobs of Stork SB from its round plastic tub ('best' butter was only used in our house on special occasions). It melted in like a snowman dying in a patch of sunshine.

Next, he would fill our mugs with tea. Three sugars each, plenty of milk. We'd tear strips off our hot toast and dunk them into the tea, savouring the milky sweet, buttery hybrid and watching a golden oil slick form in the mug of tea that was only for dipping.

*

I take a cup off the nurse's mobile tray and smile, hand it to dad.

'Do you want a digestive, Frank?' the nurse asks.

'No.' I hear the word among his babbling. I move a stray hair off his forehead. His skin is soft and warm.

Over in the corner, Mary is shouting again: 'No! No! No!' A nurse is trying to get a straw in her mouth to help her drink her tea. Dad wants to get up and help, to comfort Mary – a muscle memory from his days as a community bus driver – but I distract him.

'Remember the dipping cuppas, Dad?' I ask, and he looks down into his cup.

Food is what connects us; what often makes my belly as fat as his. As his used to be. Food is what mended our family if only superficially, papered over the cracks, kept our mouths moving when we forgot how to talk to each other.

I want to believe he's seeing the oil slick. I want to hear him say it.

But all I hear is babbling.

Frank's Hands

It comes with a walloping thump, Frank's disagreement. Frank's not wanting to put his shoes on today. Frank's weariness.

Liz sees her husband through a haze of light spots, with a *shooshing* noise in her ears that comes from her hearing aids – shocked by the unexpected jolt.

His hands, back now by his sides, once held a microphone to his rock star handsome mouth, placed a gold band on her finger, wiped their children's backsides, steered HGVs, stroked her face with tenderness and love. Covered his own face when the diagnosis came.

And now, busted her lip. Bloodied it.

His milky blue eyes blink at her; empty. Their lifelong love – his memory of it – lost in the fissure of that split.

In Dreams

'What kept you?' he asks. For it's a man – the image of your father but much younger. Skin smooth and unlined, hair jet black and lustrous like rich threads. Face open and full of life and thought. He's sitting on a tree stump beneath the canopy through which only the most determined sunlight is able to make its way.

'I've been waiting here these last two years, willing you to find me.' His voice not chiding but thick with relief. He's wearing the shirt you remember your father wearing in the photo of you and him. You as a baby and him so young and handsome, that black quiff falling into his eyes.

'The path was obscured,' you say, for you feel you need to explain. 'I didn't even know where it led. I didn't know you were here.'

'I've always been here,' he says, and he smiles the way you remember your father used to. Before he stopped smiling. Before he got old and his smile dried up with his memories.

'Your knees are bleeding,' he tells you, and you look down at them. You vaguely remember the branches scraping you as you waded through the tough undergrowth, but you don't remember pain, only the compulsion to move forward, onward.

The sight of blood on them brings to mind a picture of when you were eight and you fell off your bicycle. The only person who was able to console you was your father. He'd distracted you from the blood by giving you a choc ice and doing Dick Emery impressions: *Oh, you are awful, but I like you.* Your tears had turned to laughing, so much so that you almost threw the choc ice back up again. Your dad had wiped ice cream and tears and snot from your face, using spit and a blue striped handkerchief.

The man who looks so much like your father takes a hanky from his pocket. You see stripes, and your father's initials sewn into the corner.

'Here, let me bathe them for you,' he offers, and in your mind you're an eight-year-old boy again. And he's your dad. And he's back.

Things Frank Loves

Things Frank used to love:
- The music of Elvis Presley, Christy Moore and Mario Lanza
- Cars, *although he always bought ones that broke down after an hour*
- Food, *especially his home-made curry and cake and custard*
- Daft dad jokes. *What do you call a deer with no eyes? No idea*
- Baseball caps
- Holidays in America where he could drive for miles and miles without seeing another car. *When he first stood at the edge of the Grand Canyon, he couldn't speak for five minutes and had tears in his eyes. This was beauty he could hardly fathom, and he doesn't even know now that he's lost the concept of it*
- Football. *Stoke City*
- Caring for people

- His wife
- His children
- Family and friends
- Film and TV
- Snooker

Things Frank now loves:

- Hats. *Sometimes he'll wear two at the same time*
- Pushing his carer around in a wheelchair, *because somewhere in his DNA that caring gene is still there*
- Kicking a soft football in the lounge with one of the pretty young nurses. *Sometimes he'll kick it back to them and sometimes he won't*
- Pretty young nurses. *When he's acting up, a good-looking woman can always make him behave*
- Banana yoghurt
- Blackcurrant juice
- Cake and custard
- Walking around the maze of corridors, holding his carer's hand
- Snooker

Flounder

When I was ten, dad took me to the end of Blackpool Pier while mum and Dawn went shopping for souvenirs, and we dangled a line in the sea. It was a gorgeous summer, in the days when all summers were gorgeous because there was no school and every day seemed like an endless river of adventure.

He let me put worms on the end of the hook, telling me not to be squeamish about it. I hated the tiny pop of the sharp pin-end in their flesh, but I loved the look in dad's eyes as he watched me. I loved him so much, and he was here!

Every time he caught something the water cascaded off it like molten gold as he lifted it on to the pier. I believed he had the power to turn ordinary water into precious liquid metal and that he was doing it just for me, because he wanted my heart to burst with love and pride.

*

Today, dinner for dad is something resembling fish, at least in smell. But he's turning his nose up. It's not the same, eating mushy greying fish flesh, when you've held in your hands the pulsing heart and guts of a live fat flounder. I take his plate from him; tell him I'll ask a carer if there's something better.

As I take it, his hand brushes mine. The nut-brown has long gone and his skin is faintly purplish and translucent. I can almost see the blood inside him, and the sight stops me in my tracks. This man is still alive. I lace my fingers in his, surprised at their warmth, and each pulse of that blood brings a fresh memory.

Ba-dum, wiping blood from my knees after teaching me to ride a bike

Ba-dum, holding me in his arms and jumping into the sea screaming *Geronimo!*

Ba-dum, tying my shoelaces and telling me to be a brave boy as we put our pet dog Mick into the ground

Ba-dum, crying as he held my daughter and told me she looked like her gran

Ba-dum, asking me where Mick was fifty years after we buried him

Ba-dum, asking me where mum was when she was sitting right with us

Ba-dum, asking me who I was, and shouting to a nurse that an intruder was in his room

'What would you like, Dad?' I ask. I look into his eyes, and I want to believe he's back there, on a pier under an unseasonably blue sky, with a heavy line in the water and a ten-year-old son seeing liquid gold pour from his hands.

'Flounder,' he says, and I see those eyes twinkle like English sundrops on the Irish Sea.

Loss

This man who changed your nappies, now smells faintly of piss and has lost his false teeth. It's teatime. Relatives sit with people they once made love to, or suckled at the breast of. Loss is bleeding from them.

Pudding comes and dad returns briefly. He remembers cake. At the first spoonful he pulls his frail hand into a fist (*Yes, lovely!*) and some core cells in you want to grab his finger with your own fist and never let go.

DNR

If my condition is terminal, with no hope of recovery;
If I am unconscious with no hope of recovery;
If I am severely and permanently mentally impaired...

...I would like the following done:

i) I do not want to be kept alive by artificial life support

When Dawn's dad was forty he got a CB radio. This was in the early Eighties and it was illegal to own one, but their family lived on the edge of criminality, as Dawn's brother John would often say. He set up his station in the kitchen and amongst the steam from saucepans and the clatter of cutlery he'd talk - or copy - with people from all over the world.

'CQ, CQ, CQ DX,' was his mantra, his call to connect with people from long distances.

Her mum would stand in front of him and complain that she felt further away than the man he was talking to in Chesapeake Bay.

'It's like his bloody life support,' she'd complain, and more than once Dawn saw her eyeing up the plug to the microphone, contemplating pulling it out.

ii) I do not want to be fed by a tube

Dawn's dad was threatened with beatings if he didn't clear his plate. His father had been one of the first British soldiers to enter Bergen-Belsen concentration camp in Germany after the end of the war, and witnessed first-hand poor, skeletal souls dying at the rate of about five hundred a day. So his fucked-up view of food and eating could be excused, after listening to all those stories.

Her grandfather force-fed her father, but not with a tube. With words, with threats, with disapproval and lack of demonstrable love.

iii) I do not want to be given CPR if my heart stops beating

Dawn's dad has a big heart. A big personality. Big Frank, he's known as. Everyone loves him. Sometimes, when Dawn is in the room with him, she can almost hear his heart. She supposes that's love; sensing the rhythm of someone else's existence. Measuring her father's beats with her own. Feeling the heat of his pulse.

Knowing if it stopped, she wouldn't know what to do.

iv) If I develop another illness, I do not want treatment for that illness

'I won't be here next Christmas.'

He's said this for years. Dawn's family has heard it so often it's always been hard to tell if he is really poorly.

Now, they have no doubt.

v) If I become violent, administer behaviour-controlling drugs, even if they worsen my condition or shorten my life

Dawn gets the phone call first thing in the morning, before her head has really woken up.

'Dawn, they've taken your dad in.'

Breath taken. Blood cold. These are clichés but they're true. Six years on from the diagnosis, and a scant few months from really noticing it creeping up like a glacier, here it is.

After an aggressive episode, a Section under the Mental Health Act. Now, it's just a matter of time.

vi) If I am in pain, administer pain-killing drugs, even if they worsen my condition or shorten my life

Bruised hands from being restrained. Cracked ribs from falling. Chronic neuralgia of the face. Arthritis. Pain. Pain. Pain.

Pain-killing drugs even if they worsen his condition or shorten his life. Dawn's family roll those words around their tongues, taste the acid of them. The drugs might be doing both those things.

They see the former because he's now just lying on his bed every day and won't get up.

They pray for the latter.

The Doorway Through Which Your Heart is Destroyed

Behind Door One is your mum. Flowery apron, curlers in, holding the baby you in her lap. She has your legs in the air and she's dabbing purple lotion on your bum with cotton wool.

You move along.

Door Two opens on to darkness. There's a clock ticking, and the sound of whimpering. Your eyes adjust and you recognise the white cot. The rail bears the teeth marks left there by you and your brother before you. You both feared the dark.

Door Three is hanging off its hinges. There's mayhem behind it; the blur of a family like an old film speeded up. Kids squabbling, mother cooking, cat sicking up hairballs in the corner and Mick the dog eating them. There's no father. He's the one who knocked this door off its hinges.

Surely he'll be behind Door Four, the father. He was home sometimes. Ah, here he is. Sitting in his armchair. The year is 1971 or 1972. The year he had the moustache that grew down into a kind of Mexican affair. One of the years he smoked, certainly, when smoking seemed compulsory. Before he left? After he came back? Before he left again? Definitely one of the in-between times.

Door Five is a doctor's office. Your mum and dad (his moustache is white now) are sitting on one side of a desk, and a pleasant looking woman is asking your dad who the Prime Minister is.

Doors Six to Nine reveal rooms filled with colours, smells, noises.

The mud-brown paint the tin declared was Woodland Mushroom and that adorned your parents' bedroom walls for years; the nose-stinging smoke that always accompanied your dad's attempts at cooking; the fights, the fights, the endless fights. The pink of the roses in your wedding bouquet and the grey of your dad's suit; the smell of whisky on his breath that you noticed when you took his arm to walk down the aisle; the ringing of decades of family life and the sobs and laughter that passed down the years alongside it.

You close each of those doors with a heavy heart.

Door Ten is the door of the care home. You have to punch a code to get into this one, then walk through a few more. When you get to his room you hesitate outside, trace your fingers over the metal plate that displays his name. This is the one room you really don't want to look into. You never do. It's the doorway through which your heart is destroyed.

But you go in.

He's lying on the bed, his body now just skin on bones. He's awake so you raise the head of his bed and wash his face with a cool, damp flannel. Play music on your phone to which he sings along with his nonsense words.

His voice is sweet and quiet.

I'll Never Forget I Love You

I'll never forget I love you.

Liz chants this several times, pulls wet strands of hair off her cheek, squeezes her eyes tight shut.

She feels her feet sink lower whenever she tries to move; engulfed in swirling cold and grainy softness. It's pulling her. She doesn't want to be pulled; she wants to walk with her own will. She wants to get there herself.

Dawn persuaded her to come here because just being on a sandy beach holds memories of them all when the kids were little. Then, it had been Blackpool; Kiss-me-Quick hats and bright pink candy floss; cones of shrimps on the beach. Sun on their skin before anyone knew that was dangerous.

Today, it's Crosby Beach because Dawn has business in Liverpool and thought it would be good for them to feel the sand between their toes. Get a break from Frank; the constant visiting. Liz wants so much to empty her mind, but the one hundred cast iron men rooted in the sand make her think of nothing but the absence of her husband. Always constantly by her side and now a billion miles away. These sculptures look so much like he used to – tall and strong, full of energy and life. Their massive presence is now a hundred mockeries of his frailty.

The horizon is painted with huge ghost hulks, moving along the barely-there line with the speed of lumbering giants. She tries to imagine who is aboard. Holidaymakers on the massive liners, looking for adventure in a different place every day. The container ship captains, responsible for moving someone's whole life across continents, to make roots somewhere else.

In another place. She envies them all.

The sand here is shimmering with reflections of everything overhead, like it's a mirror showing all that could be if life wasn't so cruel. She never knew she'd end up as someone who would dread the reflections she saw. Whenever she looked in a mirror she saw a face so ravaged with lines and greyness she looked way older even than her eighty years. And in this sand now she can see her whole, miserable life. She never thought it possible to feel this much pain.

It's said drowning occurs silently, under a cloak of calm serenity. Not, as some people think, in a frenzy of waving and thrashing. Her life lately has been so much waving and thrashing. She craves the peace so much.

Liz lifts her feet out of the sand, puts one in front of the other until the water is creeping up beyond her shoes, to her ankles, sucking at her leggings. She thinks back to the early days of their marriage, lying in the warmth of the bath and the warmth of each other.

'You know I'll always love you, don't you, Liz?' he'd always say.

'Good, and don't you ever forget it.'

'I'll never forget I love you, Liz.'

But it had been a promise he couldn't keep. He's forgotten now. But she never will.

She walks further until her calves are submerged. She wants all the noise of seagulls and people and memories to stop. She wants peace and serenity to be the last things she'll ever feel.

She feels someone behind her, and they take her hand. She imagines it's Frank, but she knows it's not and the severity of that truth causes a sob to explode from her mouth.

'Come on, Mum,' Dawn says gently, quietly, and leads her from the edge of the sea.

The Thing They Don't
Talk About

They never talk about Dad's death, Dawn and her mother. Especially when he's there. They just stay silent and watch his bones become visible. Watch his skin become loose and papery, watch his face become slender and pointy and his eyes fill with fear.

They don't talk about his death even though it sits with him in his room every day, and some days it makes him stay in bed until noon, and some days it keeps him awake all night and he wanders the corridors looking for friends who left this world many years ago, and for his young children who he thought were sleeping upstairs.

They stay silent and watch death take his appetite, see it take the knowledge of how to chew and swallow. Death steals his focus, steals his dignity, steals his body's functions one by one.

They don't talk about it, even though it's advancing over the horizon like an army of cruel despots intent on annihilation, complete destruction.

Dawn wishes her mum would talk about it, but she holds on to her marriage fiercely, as she has for fifty-five years. Her wedding ring has never been off her finger, despite her having many valid reasons for taking it off through all those long years.

Today when they visit, Dad is weepy. He's babbling more than usual and he's upset about something. He grabs Liz's hand and – for once – they can hear words. 'Sorry. You have to believe me.'

'I do,' she says. 'Nothing matters. Everything before today doesn't matter.'

Dawn's not sure how true that is, but her mum wants him to believe it even if she doesn't. She wants his pain to go.

They're silent in the car on the way home, and they watch the raindrops chase each other down the windscreen. April showers. Soon the second summer since they started to say goodbye to him will be here. Neither of them has ever dared to wonder if he'll see it.

As they pull into the driveway and Dawn turns off the engine, her mum twists her wedding ring around and around.

'Let's talk about it,' she says.

Let Forever Be Now

The decline is rapid. And yet stretches endlessly.

Age is brutal. Illness is brutal. Mortality is brutal. They work like an army of renegades, set on death and destruction, and they don't care about the prisoners they take.

When he first went to hospital, he had flesh on his bones; dentures in his mouth. He had two shoes and endless socks and now everything goes missing, and his TV is on top of his wardrobe because he ripped it down from the wall.

These days he eats everything with a spoon, and gums sandwiches into submission. It takes him ages, but eventually they disappear. If – *big if* – he remembers how to swallow. Because he's forgetting how to do that.

Sometimes he forgets what a spoon is and tries to talk into it like a phone. He puts various objects to his ear to listen to them. He puts trousers on over his head. He goes to the toilet on the armchair in the bedroom next to his room, because it looks like a toilet, or like a commode, or maybe he just doesn't know where to shit anymore.

Now he's in his 'Forever Home' and the only thing you can think about is how forever is a long time. Please God, let him not live forever. Make forever now. Make forever come quickly.

Make it end now.

Don't Fear the Wolf or: The Slow Devouring of Frank

When she goes to the wardrobe to choose her outfit for her nephew's funeral, Liz finds the wolf behind her old work suits. She tries hard to ignore it, but as she selects trousers, blouse, bag, she feels its hot breath on the back of her hand. Its saliva puddles on the floor of the closet and collects in her best black court shoes, so she chooses her second best, and shuts the door. The wolf makes a slow, irritated growl.

When Frank's brain had begun to shrivel and die under the tyranny of disease, he'd told her it felt like his head was being eaten from the inside out. At night, she'd hear him scream 'Oh, the teeth! The teeth!' and he'd writhe in pain and fear while she held his head in her hands and stared into his face, trying to recognise just one thing about him before all of him disappeared.

At the funeral, the wolf sprawls beyond the coffin, with its head on its enormous paws. She checks for signs that other people see it, but no one pays any attention. It's hard to believe they can't at least smell the odour of death from its matted fur, or its awful, fetid breath.

Everyone agrees how tragic it is that Gavin was taken so soon. She tries to respond, but every time she opens her mouth, the wolf lifts its head in the air and sends a keening howl up into the rafters of the church. The sound is like madness. Yes, it's fucking unthinkable that a man in his fifties was taken. Her sister-in-law shouldn't have to bury a son.

But *she* shouldn't have to bury a husband. Not without being able to say goodbye. She's going to have to do it before too long. As well as eating his brain, the wolf has also eaten their last farewells.

She watches it padding in slow, meandering lines around the altar, down into the pews where the congregation (the oldest of whom are the same faces that had been at her wedding) are sniffing into hankies or wiping tears from their cheeks.

It's stalking her like prey. It's going to play with her like it played with Frank, and at some point, it will rip out her brains and feast on them while she's asleep.

She's not afraid. She's lived with impending death for more than a year. She's ready.

Weather

When he's happy, the sun shines, even when it's raining outside.

Dawn realises that it shines from the eyes of everyone who watches her father. When he's in the sitting room, and she's trying to spoon mashed potatoes into his mouth, they follow every move. They match his laughs with their own, smile wide when he shows his pink gums.

Every carer loves him. And everyone who loves him cares.

When he shouts and throws his potatoes on the floor, care workers appear with cloths, and they touch Dawn's arm gently, kindly.

When he's not happy, storm clouds come, behind which all in his path hide. Caught by his still strong fists, shocked by his strength, his carers silently mourn this gradual erosion of him, and Dawn and her family try to stifle the shame; try to stand upright when he shouts into their faces, shows inexplicable anger, and hurts them physically and emotionally.

Stand upright even when all they want to do is collapse.

'Hiya, Dad.' Dawn enters his room, dreading what might be in there. There's a puddle on the floor by the wardrobe, and his curtains are hanging loose off the rails.

It's quiet – neither sunshine nor storm. Her father is lying on the bed, and Dawn waits.

Waits to see what the weather will do next.

Dad-Shaped Hole

Way More Than Yog
'That yog-*hurt*!' he'd wince, putting the yoghurt on the belt. 'That cabb-*age*.' Clever word games for all occasions. Until the dementia. Now, shopping fucking hurts. Way more than yog. Because he'll never make her laugh in the aisles of Sainsbury's again, and he'll never cram all her crap into his boot and drive her home, and stop in for a cuppa and a piece of coffee cake.

First and Last
Watching him die will be a privilege. Loving someone means you don't want them to be alone right at the end. It means no matter how scary it is, or how much it hurts, NOT being there would be so much worse.

He witnessed her first breath. She'll stay until he takes his last.

Hands of Love
A soft memory brushes her hand; she can almost feel it. Whenever she was anxious, he'd assuage it,

his fingers on her palm. She aches now for what's lost. He can't comfort her anymore because he's not there. Not really. The dad she knew has become the tiniest little entity inside a cavernous empty body. Sometimes, she imagines she can even hear his little voice shouting up to be saved.

A Different Hue
Life has a 'look' now. The light is different, she thinks. She can't – doesn't want to – open her eyes fully to it. Grief has glued them shut. She never knew it was possible to grieve for someone who's still alive.

Crumple
She channels his essence to get through the tough days. What would *he* do? Laugh? Pull a face? She tries it; the mad gurning. It crumples into ugly crying.

Letting Him Go

The time is coming. You can feel it. You can see it.

His bones are all but naked now; disrobed of his flesh. There's no fat there anymore. Sometimes he responds to music and sings along to the tunes he knew from way back, but more often than not, he doesn't.

His room is always hot and the air in there is holding a secret. It knows when he's going to die. It may allow you to be there to witness it, or it may let him go when you're not there; in the dead of night or on a non-visiting day, just to be spiteful.

Because you're not in charge. Not you. Not your mother. Not your brother.

And certainly not your father.

You sit and hold his hand while he lies on his bed. That's where he always wants to be now. He's grown weary of getting up and dressed. So you sit and watch him doze, and every now and then his eyes drift open and sometimes when he sees you his pupils widen like he's seen an angel – but maybe that's your imagination – and then they close again as he drifts back to sleep.

You feel the pulse in his frail hand and count all the beats, each one seeming to tick off a memory:

The time he left home the night your mum's dad died; your family trips to the zoo; the time you saw him in town with a strange blonde woman; the day your then fiancé and you went to tell him you were getting married and he was over the moon; your wedding day when he was so nervous he got drunk but did a lovely speech, and he looked so handsome in his grey suit; your holidays in America where you rode rollercoasters and drove thousands of miles and laughed a lot; the many times you sat on his knee as a little girl; the way he called you Blossom.

And his laugh. The way he raised one eyebrow – or lowered one, it was always hard to tell. His daft jokes. His fear of not being liked. Not being loved.

His fear of Alzheimer's.

You've discovered you can be afraid of something for so long and then suddenly, the fear of it goes away. His fear of Alzheimer's went away when it took his memories. You think maybe that's the only decent thing about that fucking awful disease.

And you used to be afraid of him dying; your Daddy, your hero. You've always known he's a flawed individual, but that doesn't matter. You love him regardless and you always thought the pain of him dying would be unbearable.

But now you know there's a pain much, much worse than watching him die. It's watching him live a horrible life. It's watching him disappear and become the shell from which your father left.

It's watching him look at you and not know who you are. *That* is the most unbearable pain.

So you've decided: you're letting him go. You're going to hold his hand as long as you can. You're going to kiss his cheek and tell him you love him – even if he can't hear you – and you're going to let him go.

Only About Love

When you shave him, he moves his mouth and face around like he's chewing an invisible sweet. He offers up his neck with absolute trust; you glide the blade down beneath his chin and over his Adam's apple. It's massive, like he's swallowed a rock.

You hear the rasp of his stubble and it's almost like the noise is coming from you, because there's sandpaper inside you. Your stomach is made of it. Your heart is made of it. Your throat. Your insides have been transformed into a million tiny pieces of rock.

He can no longer speak, but words are unnecessary. Life is now simple in its cruelty; he once cared for you and now you're caring for him.

Each touch of your fingers on his skin reminds him that love still exists. You want all his waking thoughts from now on to be only about love.

Whistle Stop

There's something familiar about the whistle from his nose.

They said his breaths will become shorter, shallower. You hear it. The rattle of his hard to shift phlegm is getting quicker, his chest rising faster.

You dip the little 'lollipop' brush in the water and moisten his lips, comb the errant hairs of his untidy moustache.

Your breaths soon match his; in and out, taking in love and trying to push out fear and sorrow. You close your eyes to the pull of faux sleep, but with every cough from him, every change of breath pattern, your eyes snap open and your stomach is a mass of knots and fear. The hours stretch long. Agonisingly slow yet stealthy.

They said he'll soon start to leave longer gaps between breaths. So you listen; count the seconds, like he showed you when you were small, to see how far away the storm was. He starts to hold in air and keep it there longer and longer. You hold your breath too, finally finding the memory of that whistle – snuggled under the blanket with your cold feet at his warm back, counting the petals on the wallpaper, listening to your mum downstairs.

You remember it all. The whistle and the long, Sunday wake-up stretches he'll never do again.

You kiss his cheek, stroke him, tell him you love him. Try to forget you've not been able to communicate with him properly for almost two years, and it's killing you. The sadness of it. The sheer unfairness because it's too late now. You want to go outside and take a poor, overworked and underpaid doctor by the lapel and ask for time, some more fucking time. And for his brain to stop playing its cruel game so he can understand you. The nurses say his hearing will be the last thing to go and he'll hear you, but your heart is aching and weeping with the knowledge that hearing and understanding are not the same things. Not the same things at all.

But you talk to him anyway. Because... what if at the very end it all comes back?

'It's okay, Dad. We're here. Relax and go to sleep.'

You want to crawl into the bed with him one more time, like those long-ago Sunday treats while your mum did the housework. You want to feel the heat of him again, while it's still there.

So you hold his hand, making contact skin on skin. And you keep a hold until like the whistle, his pulse stops.

Don't let go until the warmth is gone.

Now I'm Found

'How can you be lost if you don't know where you are?'

That's always been my view, and people laugh at me, but let them. It makes sense if you really think about it. Everyone's freaking out here, and Liz has the map out, like she'll be able to help anyway. That's a laugh. Even when we're in England, she can't read maps. Has to turn them upside down whenever we're travelling south, otherwise she gets her left and right turns confused. So here in America, she has no chance.

Everyone's worried and saying we missed the turning, but I'm just eating Skittles with my left arm tanning out of the window and I'm loving it. Take a look out of that windscreen. Look ahead. How can you be worried about anything when you can see that out of your window? The horizon is so huge you can hardly believe it. They call it Big Sky country here and I can see why. You can see the very edge of the world. *All* of it. Stretching out like the whole planet is right there.

And all *my* planet *is* right here. In front of me; that pink-tinged sky with thunderheads threatening, beckoning me to some great adventure, letting me do it, feel it, experience it. I'm so lucky.

Because the rest of my planet is right here in the RV with me. My Liz, John and Dawn. My life, my absolute world. And I almost threw it away, almost lost them. Many times. Back then it was like I didn't care, but I did, I really did. It was just that some madness overcame me, some shit I couldn't handle. Some stuff from the past.

But I've learned the past sometimes tells lies to distract us from our future. It taunts us and makes us cling on to things, memories, that hold us back. It tells us lies about how important we are to people whose opinions we shouldn't care about. If you're stupid, you let it lie to you for a long time.

But if you're lucky, eventually you wake up.

The kids are adults now, with their own families, but they're here with us to celebrate our fiftieth anniversary, because they know how much I love this country and how close we came, Liz and I, to not reaching this milestone.

I keep saying it, but I'm lucky. I'm the luckiest man alive. If I were a religious man I would say I got separated from the other sheep, got lost out in a field with no grass and no life, and almost starved because the nourishment I needed was in the field I left to look for somewhere greener. But there's no grass greener than that in your own yard. There's no love like the love your own flock give you.

And it's all about love. It's *only* about love.

I'm not religious, but I feel blessed. I have my sense of priorities back. I have my family squabbling in the back about whose fault it is we missed the Pigeon Forge exit and whether we'll ever actually get to Dollywood before dark. I love it, because I nearly didn't have a family to squabble with and the sound of it, the feel of it, is like a soft blanket being wrapped around me.

I have a woman beside me who's grey like me. We always promised we'd grow old and grey together, and it's a privilege. An absolute privilege.

You can never be lost if you don't know where you're going. But the same is true if you are with the ones you love. I'm going to a beautiful future, I'm going there with Liz, and nothing and no one can stop me.

Acknowledgements

Thank you to: Urška Vidoni, Bradley Thomas and all at Fairlight Books. To Tracy Fells for wisdom, advice and friendship. Thank you to the amazing people who have kindly offered words of endorsement (Lisa Blower, Tracy Fells, Michael Loveday) – I am humbled. Love and thanks to all the people of the wonderful Flash Fiction community, especially fabulous Flash Mobsters. Thank you to my mum, Moreen Jones, who is the proudest in all the world of me. To my brothers Lee and David Jones, who may recognise slivers of truth among this fiction. To my husband Keith, for always believing in me. And to my dad, Leon Jones, the man I most wanted to see me publish my first book. He is no longer here, but if he was, and if he could understand this, it could never have been written. So this is how it has to be.

The flashes first appeared as follows: 'Breaking Dad' – Ad Hoc Fiction 2017, 'Fly Away' – Virtual Verse 2020, 'Loss' – Paragraph Planet 2018, 'The Thing They Don't Talk About' – The Writing Kiln, Potteries Prize 2nd Place 2019, 'Only About Love' – Ad Hoc Fiction 2019.

Bookclub and writers' circle notes for the
Fairlight Moderns can be found at
www.fairlightmoderns.com

Share your thoughts about the book
with #OnlyAboutLoveNovella

Also in the Fairlight Moderns series

Bottled Goods by Sophie van Llewyn

Travelling in the Dark by Emma Timpany

Atlantic Winds by William Prendiville

The Driveway Has Two Sides by Sara Marchant

There Are Things I Know by Karen B. Golightly

Inside the Bone Box by Anthony Ferner

Minutes from the Miracle City by Omar Sabbagh

The Therapist by Nial Giacomelli

The Nail House by Gregory Baines

Milton in Purgatory by Edward Vass

Missing Words by Loree Westron

Taking Flight by JT Torres

Blue Postcards by Douglas Bruton

JT TORRES

Taking Flight

When Tito is a child, his grandmother teaches
him how to weave magic around the ones
you love in order to keep them close.

She is the master and he is the pupil, exasperating
Tito's put-upon mother who is usually the focus of
their mischief.

As Tito grows older and his grandmother's mind
becomes less sound, their games take a dangerous
turn. They both struggle with a particular spell, one
that creates an illusion of illness to draw in love.
But as the lines between magic and childish tales
blur, so too do those between fantasy and reality.

'Taking Flight *is finely crafted,*
lyrical song of a book.'
—Amy Kurzweil, author of *Flying*
Couch: a graphic memoir

'The exquisite writing of JT Torres is on full
display in this deftly told and spellbinding tale.'
—Don Rearden, author of
The Raven's Gift